Angel
AND THE
POLAR
BEAR

A PANDA PICTURE BOOK

Published in 1993 by
Stoddart Publishing Co. Limited
34 Lesmill Road
Toronto, Canada
M3B 2T6
(416) 445-3333

Second printing August 1994

First published in hardcover in 1988 by
Stoddart Publishing Co. Limited

Canadian Cataloguing in Publication Data

Gay, Marie-Louise
    Angel and the polar bear

ISBN 0-7737-2166-5 (bound) ISBN 0-7736-7398-9 (pbk.)

I. Title.

PS8563.A868A63 1988   jC813'.54   C88-093089-6
PZ7.G39An 1988

Printed and bound in Hong Kong
by Book Art Inc., Toronto

Stoddart Publishing gratefully acknowledges the support of the Canada Council, Ontario Ministry of Culture and Communications, Ontario Arts Council, and Ontario Publishing Centre in the development of writing and publishing in Canada.

Angel
AND THE POLAR BEAR

For Jake the snake,

Stoddart

Every single morning when Angel wakes up
she yells, "MAMA! COME HERE!"
Angel is almost six years old.
She has a very loud voice.
And every single morning Angel's mother says,
"It's too early. Go back to sleep."
Angel's mother has a very tired voice.
Angel's father sleeps like a log.

This morning, Angel tried again.
"MAMA! COME HERE! There's a horrible ugly blue monster under my bed!"
Angel's mother yawned.
"...AND HE IS GOING TO EAT ME UP!!"
Angel's father snored.
Angel sighed and tried again."MAMA! PAPA! There's water all around my bed! Sharks too!!!"
No answer.
Then Angel heard the tiny *splash!* of a fish.

A FISH!?! Angel's eyes popped open. There *was* water all around her bed. In fact, there was water all over the apartment!
"Well!" said Angel, "what should I do now? I can't swim."
Then Angel got a good idea.

She lassoed her dresser, then carefully she crossed high above the water. From the top drawer she pulled out her flippers and her rubber giraffe and... SPLASH!!!

She paddled all the way to her parents' bedroom.

"Here I am, Mama! There weren't any sharks after all. I'm hungry."
"There's cereal on the kitchen table," mumbled Angel's mother, "don't make a mess."
So Angel splashed her way to the kitchen.
What a mess! Floating dishes, soggy cereal and goldfish in the toaster.
"I guess I'll just have a glass of milk," said Angel.

When Angel opened the refrigerator door an
incredibly cold blast of air whooshed out.
All the water froze.
Every single drop.

"Well!" said Angel, "what should I do now?"
Then Angel got another good idea. She slid to
the hall closet, put on her hockey skates
and knee pads, and skated all the way to her parents'
bedroom.
"Look Mama, I'm skating!"
"Very nice, dear. Please close the window,
it's chilly in here."

Meanwhile, back in the kitchen, a black nose...
and then an enormous white furry body slid
out of the fridge.
A polar bear!
A *gigantic* polar bear with a banana in his mouth!

"Now go eat your breakfast," said Angel's mother.
Angel did a graceful figure eight, then skated
toward the kitchen... and whizzed right back!
"MAMA! There's a polar bear in the kitchen!"
"Uh-huh."
"And he's eating a banana!"
"Yes, you can have a banana, Angel. Now, ple-e-e-ease
let me sleep."

The polar bear licked his lips and slowly waddled toward the bedroom.

"There he is, Mama," whispered Angel.
The polar bear lay down at the foot of the bed
and started nibbling at the quilt.
"Oh no! He's going to eat Mama and Papa!
What should I do?"
Then Angel got a *very* good idea.

She skated to the kitchen, slammed the fridge door shut,
climbed up onto a chair and turned the heat up. Way up.
All the ice melted, every little bit of it.
Then Angel opened the door and the water
rushed out onto the landing and down the stairs.
So did the polar bear.

Angel was eating her soggy cereal
when the doorbell rang.
"Is this your polar bear?" asked old Mr. Cantaloupe
who lived downstairs. "He was eating my doormat."
"Who is that, Angel?" asked her mother.
"It's Mr. Cantaloupe," said Angel in a small
voice, "he's bringing back the polar bear."
"How nice of him. Say thank you, Angel."

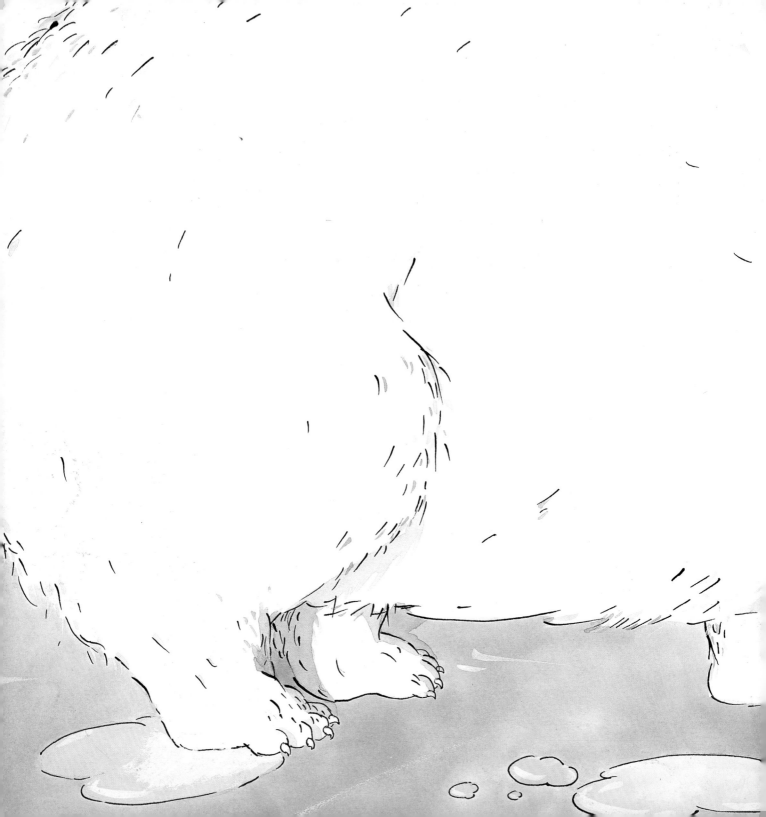

Angel stood face to face with the polar bear.
The polar bear took a giant step forward.
Angel took a tiny step backward.
The polar bear opened his mouth wide,
real wide, and growled,
"You wanna play dominoes, kid?"

So Angel and the polar bear
played dominoes.
And they ate *all* the bananas.
Every last one.